Just Like the Birdies

by Ngozi Elizabeth Mbonu

Just Like the Birdies

Copyright © 2020 by Ngozi Elizabeth Mbonu

All rights reserved.
No part of this publication may be reproduced or transmitted in any form or by any means, electronic or mechanical, including photocopy, recording, or any information storage and retrieval system, without permission in writing from the publisher.

ISBN-13: 9798572336788

Illustrations by Asim Zia. asimzia000 on Fiverr

www.cookiereads.com

This book is dedicated to
all the orphans in the world

...Be free, be your best self...

This book belongs to

I AM A COLORFUL BIRD AND I DO NOT MIND WALKING AROUND AND SHOWING OFF MY BEAUTIFUL COLORS ESPECIALLY AT THE ZOO, I REALLY DO NOT MIND PEOPLE LOOKING AT ME. THEY CAN STARE ALL DAY ACTUALLY MAKES ME FEEL PWETTY. JUST LIKE THE BEAUTIFUL PEACOCK

About the Author

Ngozi Elizabeth Mbonu is the author of four Children's books titled Tatiana, Molly the best-behaved Student, Shine, Just like the birdies, and many more to come. Ngozi Elizabeth Mbonu was born in Ottawa but spent most of her early years in West Africa. She is a microbiologist, freelance photographer, entrepreneur, enjoys traveling and meeting people.

In 2020 she moved to Kitchener, Ontario because of her love for nature. She hopes Just like the birdies will give Children a sense of liberty, freedom, and self-expression. Every Child is Unique. Her first book was turned into a movie by TIFF kids in Toronto to combat bullying among kids.

Her books have been reviewed by authorities, educators and added to library collections. You can find her books on her website http://www.cookiereads.com, she is also available on amazon platforms.

Kindly review after reading and like CookieReads on Facebook.

Manufactured by Amazon.ca
Bolton, ON